AF580285

THE STORY OF THE CLEVELAND CAVALIERS

CREATIVE EDUCATION

Published by Creative Education
123 South Broad Street
Mankato, Minnesota 56001
Creative Education is an imprint of The Creative Company.

DESIGN AND PRODUCTION BY **EVANSDAY DESIGN**

PHOTOGRAPHS BY Associated Press, AP, Getty Images (Allsport, Victor Baldizon / NBAE, Andrew D. Bernstein / NBAE, Lisa Blumenfeld, Nathaniel S. Butler / NBAE, Jonathan Daniel / Allsport, Stephen Dunn / Allsport, Focus on Sport, Jesse D. Garrabrant / NBAE, David Liam Kyle / NBAE, NBAE, Doug Pensinger / Allsport, Gregg Shamus / NBAE, Gregory Shamus / NBAE, Paul Spinelli)

Printed in the United States of America

LIBRARY OF CONGRESS CATALOGING-IN-PUBLICATION DATA

LeBoutillier, Nate.
The story of the Cleveland Cavaliers / by Nate LeBoutillier.
p. cm. — (The NBA—a history of hoops)
Includes index.
ISBN-13: 978-1-58341-403-3
1. Cleveland Cavaliers (Basketball team)—History—Juvenile literature. I. Title. II. Series.

GV885.52.C57L43 2006
796.323'64'097713—dc22 2005051206

First edition

9 8 7 6 5 4 3 2 1

COVER PHOTO: *LeBron James*

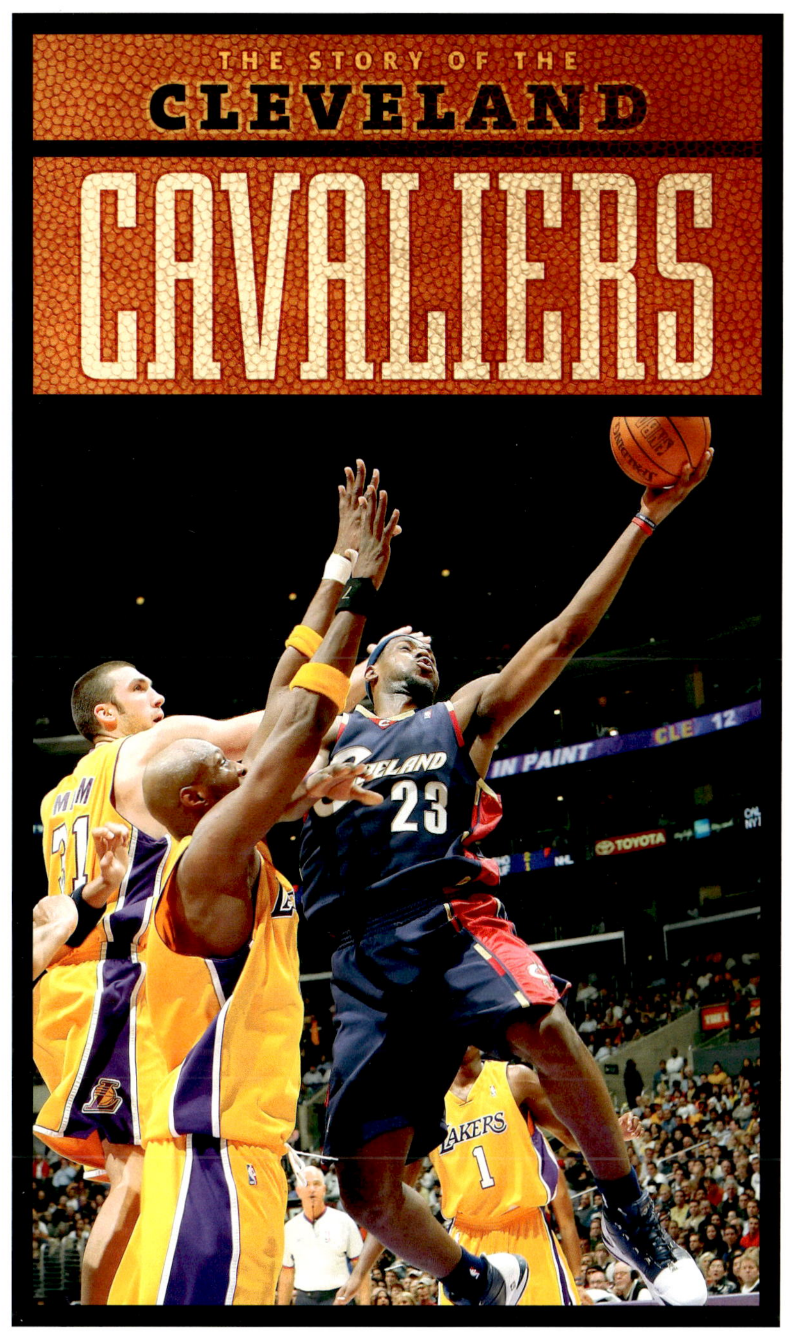

NATE LeBOUTILLIER

CREATIVE EDUCATION

23
MAGIC
9
GEICO GEICO GEICO

There's a new Number 23

DOMINATING THE COURTS OF THE NATIONAL BASKETBALL ASSOCIATION (NBA). CLEVELAND CAVALIERS FANS CHEER AS NUMBER 23 MAKES A BRILLIANT PASS TO A TEAMMATE FOR AN EASY TWO POINTS. THE FANS SCREAM AND WHISTLE AS NUMBER 23 CLIMBS AN AIR LADDER TO BLOCK A SHOT ON DEFENSE. AND WHEN NUMBER 23 SOARS FOR A SWOOPING SLAM DUNK, FANS SIMPLY GO WILD. HE LOOKS A LOT LIKE THE NBA'S OLD FAMOUS "NUMBER 23," MICHAEL JORDAN, BUT THE NEW NUMBER 23'S NAME IS LEBRON JAMES, AND HE IS READY TO BRING BASKETBALL GLORY TO CLEVELAND.

CLEVELAND CAVALIERS
Cleveland Ohio

BLUE-COLLAR BEGINNINGS

1

SITUATED ALONG THE SHORES OF LAKE ERIE, Cleveland, Ohio, has long been a community of great industrial might. For more than 140 years, the city's shipyards and railroads have helped to supply America with raw materials—including steel, coal, and aluminum. The people of Cleveland have always embraced their city's blue-collar history. Since 1970, the hardworking people of Cleveland have had an NBA team called the Cavaliers to take their minds off of work during the winter months.

The Cavaliers entered the NBA in 1970 as one of three new expansion teams, along with the Portland Trail Blazers and Buffalo Braves. The first group of Cleveland Cavaliers was a collection of aging veterans and raw rookies. After looking over his team's uninspiring roster, head coach Bill Fitch joked to the press, "Remember, my name is Fitch, not Houdini."

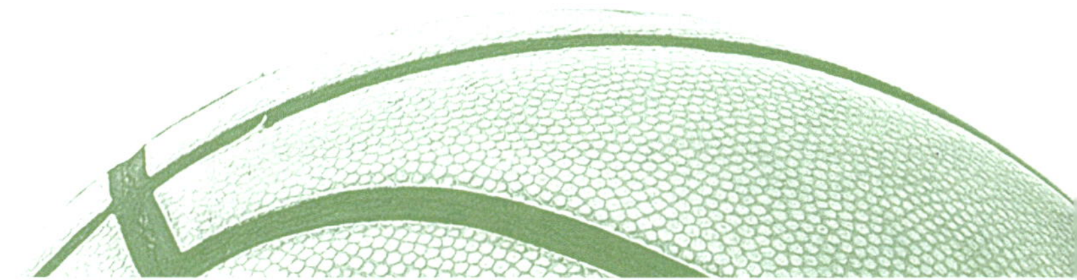

Austin Carr played nine seasons in Cleveland, netting 10,265 points—the second-most in club history

THAT HOOPS

Sometimes called "Mr. Moves," forward Campy Russell was an early Cavs standout and fan favorite

Unfortunately, Coach Fitch didn't have any magic tricks that could keep the Cavaliers from posting a woeful 15–67 mark in 1970–71. Although the team's record was poor, Cleveland discovered a few talented players—most notably forwards Bobby "Bingo" Smith and John Johnson—who would play big roles in its future.

In 1971, Cleveland used its first-round pick in the NBA Draft to choose All-American guard Austin Carr from the University of Notre Dame. Carr immediately added much-needed scoring punch to the lineup. "Every team needs a go-to guy, and we hope Austin will be ours," said Fitch. Carr struggled with a broken foot but still managed to net 21 points per game in his rookie year.

In 1974, the Cavaliers used another high draft pick to add 6-foot-8 forward Michael "Campy" Russell to the lineup. With Russell, Smith, Carr, and rugged forward Jim Chones, Cleveland finally had enough talent to contend for a playoff spot. Unfortunately, Carr injured his knee early in the 1974–75 season, and the Cavaliers went 40–42, just missing the playoffs.

THE MIRACLE OF RICHFIELD

Twenty miles south of the city of Cleveland lies the suburb of Richfield, home of the Coliseum, where the Cavaliers played from 1974 until 1994. Cavs fans have especially fond memories of the 1975–76 season in the Coliseum—a season some called the "Miracle of Richfield." In the 1976 playoffs, Cleveland battled the powerful Washington Bullets in an epic series that concluded with Game 7 in Richfield, where the underdog Cavs won, 87–85, in front of 21,564 screaming fans. "The fans would get rolling a half-hour before the game," said Cavs guard Austin Carr. "By the time we got to the court, they'd be stomping on the floor, *LET'S GO CAVS! LET'S GO CAVS!* It was to the point where the entire building was shaking. It was unbelievable, and that's how it went *every* game."

FIRST TASTE OF THE PLAYOFFS

THE CAVALIERS ENTERED THE 1975–76 SEASON determined to make the playoffs. Early in the year, Coach Fitch swung a trade that brought All-Star center Nate Thurmond to Cleveland. Although the veteran Thurmond was no longer in his prime, his forceful personality and presence in the low post were just what the young Cavaliers needed.

With Thurmond patrolling the paint, the ball-sharing Cavaliers rolled up a 49–33 record and a Central Division championship. In the first round of the playoffs, Cleveland eliminated the favored Washington Bullets in an exciting seven-game series that fans dubbed the "Miracle of Richfield." Up next were the mighty Boston Celtics. Although many experts expected Cleveland to win, the Cavs' leading scorer, Chones, broke his foot during practice and missed the entire series, and the Celtics prevailed in six games.

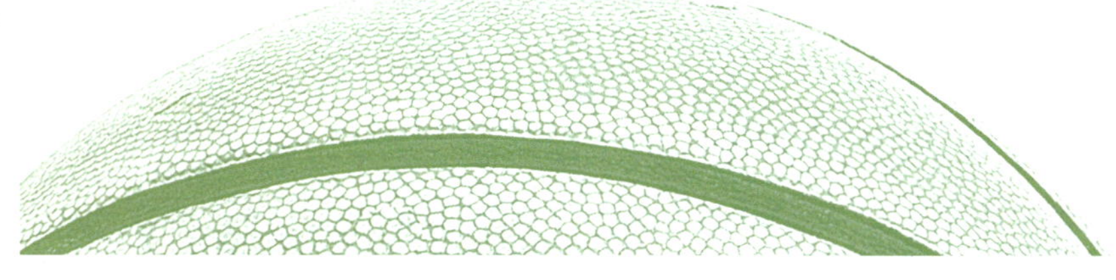

CLEVELAND

CAVALIERS

Do-it-all center Nate Thurmond spent the last two seasons of his Hall of Fame career in Cleveland

Famed for his wild but accurate shots, World B. Free averaged 23 points a game during his Cavs career

The Cavaliers marched to the playoffs each of the next two seasons but were eliminated in the first round each time. By 1979, Thurmond had retired, and veterans such as Smith and Chones were beginning to slow down. After Cleveland limped to a 30–52 record and missed the playoffs in 1978–79, Fitch stepped down as head coach.

From 1980–81 to 1983–84, Cleveland lost more than 50 games every season and went through six head coaches. As the losses piled up, attendance dropped sharply. Still, there were bright spots. Small forward Mike Mitchell used an accurate shooting eye and great leaping ability to average 19 points a game during four seasons in Cleveland. Shooting guard World B. Free, meanwhile, specialized in long-range bombing, and he rarely passed on an opportunity to fire away. "World sincerely believes every shot he takes will go in," laughed Cavs guard John Bagley. "A lot of times, he's right."

CAVS FASHION

Fashion is always changing, and fashion in the NBA is no exception. Since 1970, the Cavaliers have changed their uniforms nine times. The first Cleveland uniforms were wine- (brownish-red) and gold-colored and classically designed, but in 1983, the team's colors changed to burnt orange, white, and royal blue. The styles and color shades kept changing until 2003, when the Cavs went back to their roots—wine and gold—and implemented an updated logo design. The Cavs roster was also "redesigned" that year to include Ohio native LeBron James, and James's number 23 Cavaliers jersey quickly rocketed to the top of the NBA's best-selling apparel list. Said then-owner Gordon Gund of the new look: "We set out to have colors, logos, and uniforms that reflect our history and look forward at the same time."

THE CAVS ARE REBORN

IN 1983, BUSINESSMAN GORDON GUND PURCHASED the Cavaliers and told Cleveland fans that a new era was about to begin. "We can't promise miracles overnight," he said, "but we can promise that we are going to build a winner in Cleveland."

Gund hired former Cavs guard Lenny Wilkens as the team's new coach in 1986. Wilkens had led the Seattle SuperSonics to an NBA title in 1979, and he wasted little time in rebuilding the Cavs. With the team's top two picks in the 1986 NBA Draft, Wilkens selected 6-foot-11 and 250-pound center Brad Daugherty and explosive guard Ron Harper. Cleveland also made a draft-day deal for outstanding point guard Mark Price.

Big center Brad Daugherty surprised many an opponent with his nimble feet and soft shooting touch

Ron Harper was known as a scoring machine early in his career and a defensive whiz in his later seasons

Almost immediately, the team's fortunes rose. Daugherty's rock-steady play in the pivot perfectly complemented Harper's high-flying athleticism, and Price made opponents pay with lethal three-point shooting. Coach Wilkens and his trio of young stars got a boost when the team traded for talented veteran forwards Larry Nance and Mike Sanders late in 1987–88. The Cavaliers finished that season with a record of 42–40—their first winning mark in 10 seasons—and were suddenly a team to be reckoned with.

In 1988–89, the Cavs enjoyed their best season ever, going 57–25. In the playoffs, they faced the Chicago Bulls and their superstar, Michael Jordan. The teams fought to a two-games-to-two tie before Jordan hit a game-winning buzzer-beater in the series-deciding Game 5 in Cleveland, stunning Cavs fans into silence. The loss was a terrible blow, but the youthful Cavaliers were certain there would be more chances. "Our best days are ahead of us," Price said.

After suffering a rash of injuries the next two seasons, the Cavs rose again in 1991–92. After another 57–25 regular season, Cleveland drove all the way to the Eastern Conference Finals, where it once again faced the Chicago Bulls. The two old foes battled fiercely for six games before the Bulls triumphed. The next year, after Chicago again topped Cleveland in the playoffs, Lenny Wilkens stepped down as head coach.

Smart and steady point guard Mark Price set many of Cleveland's assist and three-point shooting records

JORDAN SINKS THE CAVS

Clevelanders have endured many bitter sports losses throughout the years. The Cavaliers' most famous downfall came against the Chicago Bulls on May 8, 1989. It was the first round of the playoffs and the fifth and deciding game of the series. Things looked good for the Cavs when guard Craig Ehlo made a lay-up with just three seconds remaining, giving Cleveland a 100–99 lead. But following a timeout, Bulls star Michael Jordan burst free to get the ball and then hit a double-clutch, 15-foot jump shot over Ehlo's outstretched fingertips. As Cleveland fans slumped in their seats, Jordan jumped around the floor in celebration. "That was uncharacteristic of me," said Jordan, who scored 44 points. "But [the fans] had been on me all day yelling 'choke' and telling me to get a tee time."

FRATELLO WINS WITH DEFENSE

4

MIKE FRATELLO WAS INSTALLED AS CLEVELAND'S head coach in 1993. While coaching the Atlanta Hawks in the late 1980s and early '90s, Fratello had earned a reputation as a great motivator. But bad health plagued the Cavs. Following the 1993–94 season, which saw Daugherty, Price, and Nance miss a bulge of games due to injury, back problems forced Daugherty—a five-time All-Star—to retire at the age of 30. Nance called it quits, too, and Price would last just one more season.

Small but fiery coach Mike Fratello guided the Cavaliers to the postseason four times in six seasons

Brevin Knight opened eyes with an 18-point, 3-steal performance in his very first NBA game in 1997

To keep the Cavs in contention, Fratello turned to an unspectacular but hardworking crew. Players such as forward Danny Ferry and guards Terrell Brandon and Bobby Phills did not give Cleveland the offensive firepower of their predecessors, but they made up for it by embracing Fratello's defensive philosophy.

Cleveland's strategy involved slowing the game down. The Cavs of the mid-1990s walked the ball up the court and patiently moved the ball around, waiting for a good shot to present itself. On defense, the team played a swarming style. Cleveland's approach wasn't exciting, but it was effective. The Cavs posted winning records each year from 1993–94 to 1996–97 and were the league's stingiest defensive team, allowing fewer than 90 points per game on average. "I'd rather win ugly than lose pretty," Coach Fratello said. Cleveland earned postseason berths in its first three seasons under Fratello but was eliminated in the first round each time.

In 1997, the Cavaliers made a major effort to improve their offense. Brandon and Phills had moved on, and in their place, the team added two talented rookies—speedy guard Brevin Knight and 7-foot-3 center Zydrunas Ilgauskas. Cleveland also traded for All-Star power forward Shawn Kemp, formerly with the Seattle SuperSonics. In 1997–98, Kemp and Ilgauskas combined for nearly 32 points and 18 rebounds per game. The Cavs finished 47–35 but were quickly eliminated in the playoffs by the Indiana Pacers.

OHIO'S NATIVE SON

INJURIES, COACHING CHANGES, AND LOSING RECORDS marred the Cavs' next five seasons. But after finishing 29–53 in 2002–03, the Cavs got lucky, winning the first pick in the NBA Draft. With it, they selected native Ohioan LeBron James, a dazzling guard who went on to earn Rookie of the Year honors and draw comparisons to the great Michael Jordan.

In 2004–05, behind a healthy Ilgauskas, the ferocious in-the-paint work of forward Drew Gooden, and the explosive James, the Cavs started out 30–20 and appeared primed to barge into the playoffs once again. But a 12–20 record down the stretch left them out of the playoffs, a bitter disappointment to James. "I take full credit," said the young superstar, following a season in which he averaged more than 27 points, 7 rebounds, and 7 assists a game. "I am the leader of this team."

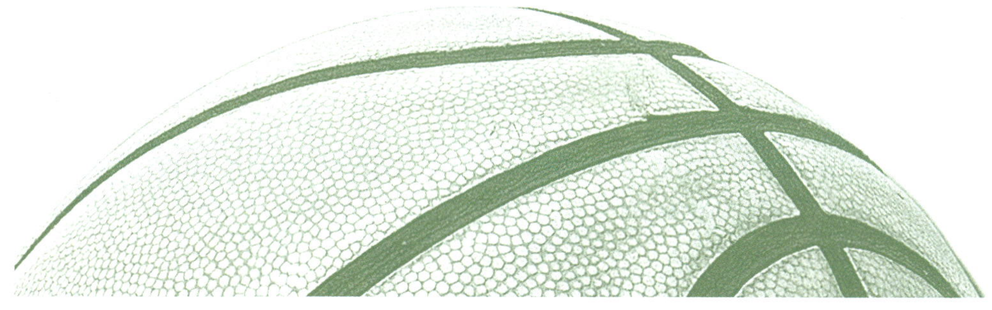

CLEVELAND CAVALIERS

Some experts believed that LeBron James had the potential to become the best player in NBA history

Hardworking forward Drew Gooden was the Cavs' best rebounder in 2004–05, snaring nine boards a game

The Cavs franchise came under new ownership in March 2005, and chairman Dan Gilbert wasted no time in shaking things up. Coach Paul Silas and general manager Jim Paxson were fired, and in the off-season, Mike Brown took over as head coach, and former Cavs player Danny Ferry was hired to replace Paxson. The moves seemed to help as the Cavs signed versatile guard Larry Hughes and locked up Ilgauskas with a new, long-term contract. Such moves had Gilbert confident that Cleveland would soon be cheering for a winner. "We believe it will be a golden era of basketball for the fans and community of this hardworking and well-deserving town," he said.

With a rebuilding effort well underway and the NBA's new Number 23 dunking, passing, and shooting his way into the top tier of NBA players, Cleveland sports fans have a lot to look forward to. At the very least, Cavs fans know that their team will fight on in the Cleveland tradition of hard work in hopes of winning that first NBA championship.

THE DRAFTING OF KING JAMES

Many Cleveland basketball fans believe that June 26, 2003, was the finest day in Cavaliers basketball history. On that day, the Cavs drafted high school phenom LeBron James in the NBA Draft. The Cavs didn't have to look any farther than their own backyard for the best prospect. James grew up in Akron and had been named Mr. Basketball of Ohio his sophomore, junior, and senior years of high school, winning three Ohio state titles. James, a lifelong Cavs fan, made the choice look good, leading the Cavs in scoring in his first three seasons despite high expectations and a circus-like atmosphere around him. "I don't need too much," said James. "Glamour and all that stuff don't excite me. I am just glad I have the game of basketball in my life."

INDEX

NBA